THE YESTE

Reycraft Books
55 Fifth Avenue
New York, NY 10003

Reycraftbooks.com

Reycraft Books is a trade imprint and trademark of Newmark Learning, LLC.

Text and illustration copyright © 2020 by Pam Fong

Educators and Librarians: Our books may be purchased in bulk for promotional, educational, or business use. Please contact sales@reycraftbooks.com.

Library of Congress Control Number: 2020908306

ISBN: 978-1-4788-6952-8

Printed in Dongguan, China. 8557/0720/17254

10 9 8 7 6 5 4 3 2 1

First Edition Hardcover published by Reycraft Books

ROU
AND THE
GREAT
RACE

PAM FONG

There came a time when
flowers
could no longer be found.

When the city started to grow,
the Power People

collected all the remaining *flowers*.

And kept them ...

... for themselves.

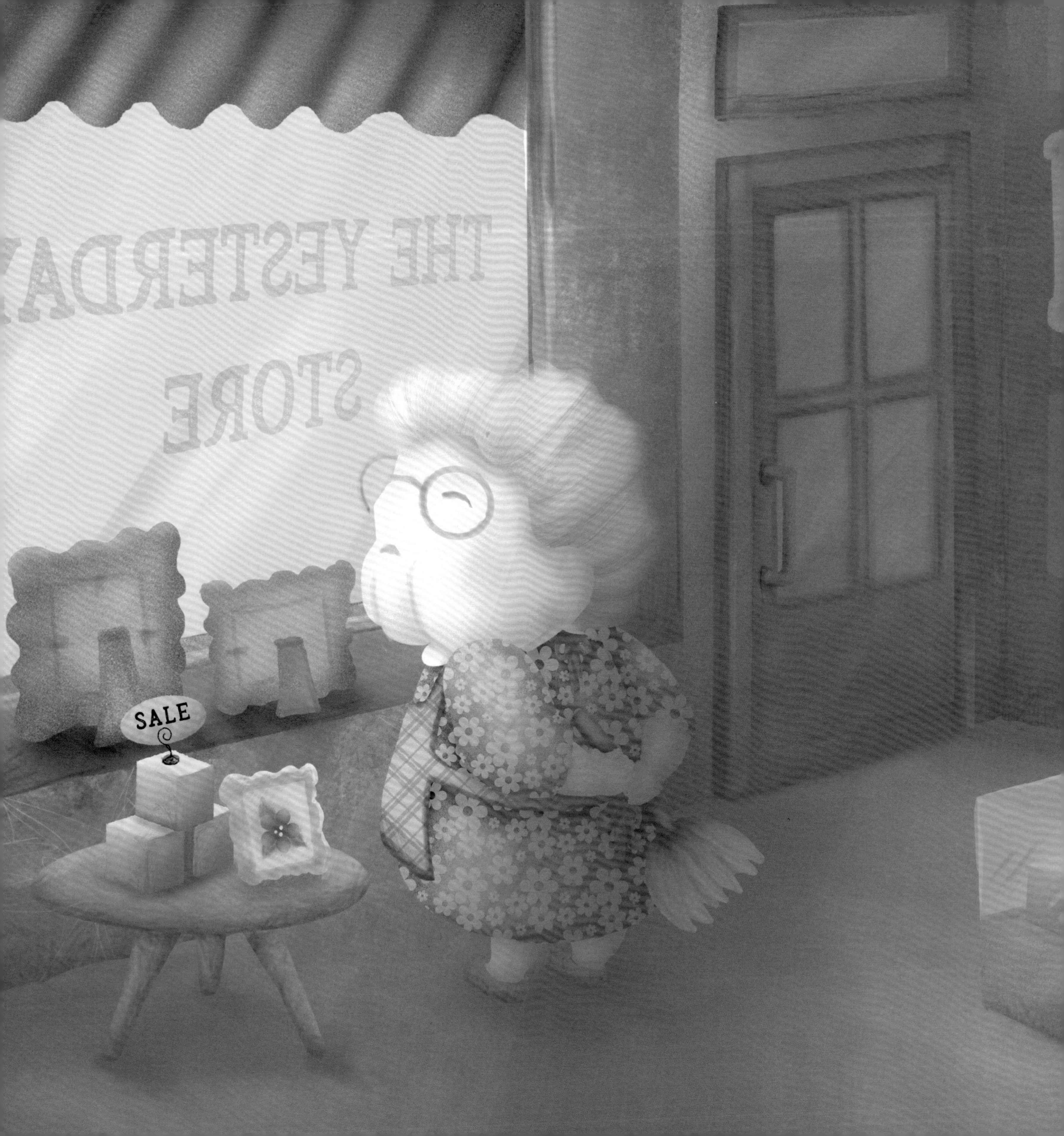
SALE

Rou's grandmother
remembered the days
when it was different.

Every night, Grandma talked about

flowers.

Her voice changed whenever she
recalled their sweet smell.

Each year, the **Power People** shared a single plant with the whole city.

KEEP OUT!

And everyone waited for it to bloom.

And when it did, they announced the date of

THE GREAT RACE.

All the children were invited to run, but only the
fastest to reach the $flower$ would get to keep it.

"This year, I will enter the race," thought Rou.

"And I know I can **win**."

Rou thought of nothing else day
and night but winning the race ...

... and the look on Grandma's face
when she surprised her with the

flower.

At last, it was the big day ...

READY.

SET.

GO!

"I didn't even get to see the flower," thought Rou.

"But what's this?"

The next year, Rou decided not to run in

THE GREAT RACE.

Instead, she stayed home …

... to help Grandma with her new

garden.

FOR MOM & DAD
who gave me every opportunity to run.

FOR PHILIPPE
who waits lovingly at every finish line.

FOR JUSTIN & ELLIOT
who remind me every day how much I have won.

–PAM